Disney
WRECK-IT RALPH

Game On!

By Susan Amerikaner

Illustrated by the Disney Storybook Artists

Random House 🏠 New York

in a video game.

Ralph wrecks things.

Wrecking is his job.

Felix fixes things
with his magic hammer.

Felix always
wins a medal.
Ralph never
gets a medal.

Bad Guys do not
get medals.
Ralph wants
to be a Good Guy.

One day,
Ralph jumps
into a new game.

He gets a medal!

Ralph goes

to <u>Sugar Rush</u> next.

It is a racing game
in a candy world.

A little girl
takes Ralph's medal!
Her name is
Vanellope.
She is in a tree.

Ralph climbs the tree.

He wants

his medal back.

Vanellope wants to be
in the <u>Sugar Rush</u> race.
She needs a gold coin
to enter.
She uses Ralph's medal.

The winner will get
all the gold coins—
and Ralph's medal!

The other racers
do not want Vanellope
to race.

They wreck
her race kart.
They throw her
in the mud.

Ralph chases them away.
He will help Vanellope
win the race.
Then she will give
Ralph his medal back!

Ralph and Vanellope
make a new race kart.

King Candy tricks Ralph.
"Vanellope will get hurt
in the race,"
he says.

Ralph cannot
let Vanellope race!
The king gives Ralph
the gold medal.

Vanellope gives Ralph
a new medal.
She made it for him.

You're My hero

Ralph wants

to save Vanellope.

He wrecks her kart.

She cannot race.

She cannot get hurt.

Vanellope is sad.
King Candy
locks her
in a cell.

Ralph wrecks the wall.

He frees Vanellope.

Felix comes
to <u>Sugar Rush</u>.
Ralph and Felix
fix Vanellope's kart.

She wins the race!

Vanellope turns
into a princess!
She is the real ruler
of <u>Sugar Rush</u>.

Vanellope just wants
to be herself.
She thanks Ralph
for his help.

Ralph goes back
to his game.
He does not need a medal
to be a Good Guy.